Roman

Joseph Conrad

This is a work of fiction. Names, characters, organizations, places, events, and incidents are either products of the author's imagination or are used fictitiously. Any resemblance of actual persons, living or dead, or actual events is purely coincidental.

No part of this work may be reproduced, or stored in a retrieval system, or transmitted in any form or by any means, electronic, mechanical, photocopying, recording, or otherwise, without express permission of the publisher.

Prince Roman by Joseph Conrad
First Published: 1920
Cover Image: An Evening beside Lake Areso
Artist: Johan Thomas Lundbye
Date: 1837
Credit Line: MET Museum, Gift of Eugene V. Thaw, 2007
License: CC0 1.0 Universal (CC0 1.0)

Published by Digibooks OOD / Demetra Publishing, Bulgaria.

All rights reserved.

Contact: info@demetrapublishing.com

ISBN: 9798633106633

PRINCE ROMAN

"Events which happened seventy years ago are perhaps rather too far off to be dragged aptly into a mere conversation. Of course the year 1831 is for us an historical date, one of these fatal years when in the presence of the world's passive indignation and eloquent sympathies we had once more to murmur '*Vo Victis*' and count the cost in sorrow. Not that we were ever very good at calculating, either, in prosperity or in adversity. That's a lesson we could never learn, to the great exasperation of our enemies who have bestowed upon us the epithet of Incorrigible...."

The speaker was of Polish nationality, that nationality not so much alive as surviving, which persists in thinking, breathing, speaking, hoping, and suffering in its grave, railed in by a million of bayonets and triple-sealed with the seals of three great empires.

The conversation was about aristocracy. How did this, nowadays discredited, subject come up? It is some years ago now and the precise recollection has faded. But I remember that it was not considered practically as an ingredient in the social mixture; and I verily believed that we arrived at that subject through some exchange of ideas about patriotism — a somewhat discredited sentiment, because the delicacy of our humanitarians regards it as a relic of barbarism. Yet neither the great Florentine painter who closed his eyes in death thinking of his city, nor St. Francis blessing with his last breath the town of Assisi, were barbarians. It requires a certain greatness of soul to interpret patriotism worthily — or else a sincerity of feeling denied to the vulgar refinement of modern thought which cannot understand the august simplicity of a sentiment proceeding from the very nature of things and men.

The aristocracy we were talking about was the very highest, the great families of Europe, not impoverished, not converted, not liberalized, the most distinctive and specialized class of all classes, for which even ambition itself does not exist among the usual incentives to activity and regulators of conduct.

The undisputed right of leadership having passed away from them, we judged that their great fortunes, their cosmopolitanism brought about by wide alliances, their elevated station, in which there is so little to gain and so much to lose, must make their position difficult in times of political commotion or national upheaval. No longer born to command — which is the very essence of aristocracy — it becomes difficult for them to do aught else but hold aloof from the great movements of popular passion.

We had reached that conclusion when the remark about far-off events was made and the date of 1831 mentioned. And the speaker continued:

"I don't mean to say that I knew Prince Roman at that remote time. I begin to feel pretty ancient, but I am not so ancient as that. In fact Prince Roman was married the very year my father was born. It was in 1828; the 19th Century was young yet and the Prince was even younger than the century, but I don't know exactly by how much. In any case his was an early marriage. It was an ideal alliance from every point of view. The girl was young and beautiful, an orphan heiress of a great name and of a great fortune. The Prince, then an officer in the Guards and distinguished amongst his fellows by something reserved and reflective in his character, had fallen headlong in love with her beauty, her charm, and the serious qualities of her mind and heart. He was a rather silent young man; but his glances, his bearing, his whole person expressed his absolute devotion to the woman of his choice, a devotion which she returned in her own frank and fascinating manner.

"The flame of this pure young passion promised to burn for ever; and for a season it lit up the dry, cynical atmosphere of the great world of St. Petersburg. The

Emperor Nicholas himself, the grandfather of the present man, the one who died from the Crimean War, the last perhaps of the Autocrats with a mystical belief in the Divine character of his mission, showed some interest in this pair of married lovers. It is true that Nicholas kept a watchful eye on all the doings of the great Polish nobles. The young people leading a life appropriate to their station were obviously wrapped up in each other; and society, fascinated by the sincerity of a feeling moving serenely among the artificialities of its anxious and fastidious agitation, watched them with benevolent indulgence and an amused tenderness.

"The marriage was the social event of 1828, in the capital. Just forty years afterwards I was staying in the country house of my mother's brother in our southern provinces.

"It was the dead of winter. The great lawn in front was as pure and smooth as an alpine snowfield, a white and feathery level sparkling under the sun as if sprinkled with diamond-dust, declining gently to the lake — a long, sinuous piece of frozen water looking bluish and more solid than the earth. A cold brilliant sun glided low above an undulating horizon of great folds of snow in which the villages of Ukrainian peasants remained out of sight, like clusters of boats hidden in the hollows of a running sea. And everything was very still.

"I don't know now how I had managed to escape at eleven o'clock in the morning from the schoolroom. I was a boy of eight, the little girl, my cousin, a few months younger than myself, though hereditarily more quick-tempered, was less adventurous. So I had escaped alone; and presently I found myself in the great stone-paved hall, warmed by a monumental stove of white tiles, a much more pleasant locality than the schoolroom, which for some reason or other, perhaps hygienic, was always kept at a low temperature.

"We children were aware that there was a guest staying in the house. He had arrived the night before just as we were being driven off to bed. We broke back through the line of beaters to rush and flatten our noses against the dark window panes; but we were too late to see him alight. We had only watched in a ruddy glare the big travelling carriage on sleigh-runners harnessed with six horses, a black mass against the snow, going off to the stables, preceded by a horseman carrying a blazing ball of tow and resin in an iron basket at the end of a long stick swung from his saddle bow. Two stable boys had been sent out early in the afternoon along the snow-tracks to meet the expected guest at dusk and light his way with these road torches. At that time, you must remember, there was not a single mile of railways in our southern provinces. My little cousin and I had no knowledge of trains and engines, except from picture-books, as of things rather vague, extremely remote, and not particularly interesting unless to grownups who travelled abroad.

"Our notion of princes, perhaps a little more precise, was mainly literary and had a glamour reflected from the light of fairy tales, in which princes always appear young, charming, heroic, and fortunate. Yet, as well as any other children, we could draw a firm line between the real and the ideal. We knew that princes were historical personages. And there was some glamour in that fact, too. But what had driven me to roam cautiously over the house like an escaped prisoner was the hope of snatching an interview with a special friend of mine, the head forester, who generally came to make his report at that time of the day, I yearned for news of a certain wolf. You know, in a country where wolves are to be found, every winter almost brings forward an individual eminent by the audacity of his misdeeds, by his more perfect wolfishness — so to speak. I wanted to hear some new thrilling tale of that wolf — perhaps the dramatic story of his death....

"But there was no one in the hall.

"Deceived in my hopes, I became suddenly very much depressed. Unable to slip back in triumph to my studies I elected to stroll spiritlessly into the billiard room where certainly I had no business. There was no one there either, and I felt very lost and desolate under its high ceiling, all alone with the massive English billiard table which seemed, in heavy, rectilinear silence, to disapprove of that small boy's intrusion.

"As I began to think of retreat I heard footsteps in the adjoining drawing room; and, before I could turn tail and flee, my uncle and his guest appeared in the doorway. To run away after having been seen would have been highly improper, so I stood my ground. My uncle looked surprised to see me; the guest by his side was a spare man, of average stature, buttoned up in a black frock coat and holding himself very erect with a stiffly soldier-like carriage. From the folds of a soft white cambric neck-cloth peeped the points of a collar close against each shaven cheek. A few wisps of thin gray hair were brushed smoothly across the top of his bald head. His face, which must have been beautiful in its day, had preserved in age the harmonious simplicity of its lines. What amazed me was its even, almost deathlike pallor. He seemed to me to be prodigiously old. A faint smile, a mere momentary alteration in the set of his thin lips acknowledged my blushing confusion; and I became greatly interested to see him reach into the inside breastpocket of his coat. He extracted therefrom a lead pencil and a block of detachable pages, which he handed to my uncle with an almost imperceptible bow.

"I was very much astonished, but my uncle received it as a matter of course. He wrote something at which the other glanced and nodded slightly. A thin wrinkled hand — the hand was older than the face — patted my cheek and then rested on my head lightly. An un-ringing voice, a voice as colourless as the face itself, issued from his sunken lips, while the eyes, dark and still, looked down at me kindly.

"'And how old is this shy little boy?'"

"Before I could answer my uncle wrote down my age on the pad. I was deeply impressed. What was this ceremony? Was this personage too great to be spoken to? Again he glanced at the pad, and again gave a nod, and again that impersonal, mechanical voice was heard: 'He resembles his grandfather.'

"I remembered my paternal grandfather. He had died not long before. He, too, was prodigiously old. And to me it seemed perfectly natural that two such ancient and venerable persons should have known each other in the dim ages of creation before my birth. But my uncle obviously had not been aware of the fact. So obviously that the mechanical voice explained: 'Yes, yes. Comrades in '31. He was one of those who knew. Old times, my dear sir, old times....'

"He made a gesture as if to put aside an importunate ghost. And now they were both looking down at me. I wondered whether anything was expected from me. To my round, questioning eyes my uncle remarked: 'He's completely deaf.' And the unrelated, inexpressive voice said: 'Give me your hand.'

"Acutely conscious of inky fingers I put it out timidly. I had never seen a deaf person before and was rather startled. He pressed it firmly and then gave me a final pat on the head.

"My uncle addressed me weightily: 'You have shaken hands with Prince Roman S —— —— -. It's something for you to remember when you grow up.'

"I was impressed by his tone. I had enough historical information to know vaguely that the Princes S —— —— - counted amongst the sovereign Princes of Ruthenia till the union of all Ruthenian lands to the kingdom of Poland, when they became great Polish magnates, sometime at the beginning of the 15th Century. But what concerned me most was the failure of the fairy-tale glamour. It was shocking to discover a prince who was deaf, bald, meagre, and so prodigiously old. It never occurred to me that this imposing and disappointing man had been young, rich, beautiful; I could not know that he had been happy in the felicity of an ideal marriage uniting two young hearts, two great names and two great fortunes; happy with a happiness which, as in fairy tales, seemed destined to last for ever....

"But it did not last for ever. It was fated not to last very long even by the measure of the days allotted to men's passage on this earth where enduring happiness is only found in the conclusion of fairy tales. A daughter was born to them and shortly afterwards, the health of the young princess began to fail. For a time she bore up with smiling intrepidity, sustained by the feeling that now her existence was necessary for the happiness of two lives. But at last the husband, thoroughly alarmed by the rapid changes in her appearance, obtained an unlimited leave and took her away from the capital to his parents in the country.

"The old prince and princess were extremely frightened at the state of their beloved daughter-in-law. Preparations were at once made for a journey abroad. But it seemed as if it were already too late; and the invalid herself opposed the project with gentle obstinacy. Thin and pale in the great armchair, where the insidious and obscure nervous malady made her appear smaller and more frail every day without effacing the smile of her eyes or the charming grace of her wasted face, she clung to her native land and wished to breathe her native air. Nowhere else could she expect to get well so quickly, nowhere else would it be so easy for her to die.

"She died before her little girl was two years old. The grief of the husband was terrible and the more alarming to his parents because perfectly silent and dry-eyed. After the funeral, while the immense bareheaded crowd of peasants surrounding the private chapel on the grounds was dispersing, the Prince, waving away his friends and relations, remained alone to watch the masons of the estate closing the family vault. When the last stone was in position he uttered a groan, the first sound of pain which had escaped from him for days, and walking away with lowered head shut himself up again in his apartments.

"His father and mother feared for his reason. His outward tranquillity was appalling to them. They had nothing to trust to but that very youth which made his despair so self-absorbed and so intense. Old Prince John, fretful and anxious, repeated: 'Poor Roman should be roused somehow. He's so young.' But they could find nothing to rouse him with. And the old princess, wiping her eyes, wished in her heart he were young enough to come and cry at her knee.

"In time Prince Roman, making an effort, would join now and again the family circle. But it was as if his heart and his mind had been buried in the family vault with the wife he had lost. He took to wandering in the woods with a gun, watched over secretly by one of the keepers, who would report in the evening that 'His Serenity has never fired a shot all day.' Sometimes walking to the stables in the morning he would order in subdued tones a horse to be saddled, wait switching his boot till it was led up to him, then mount without a word and ride out of the gates at a walking pace. He would be gone all day. People saw him on the roads looking neither to the right nor to the left, white-faced, sitting rigidly in the saddle like a horseman of stone on a living mount.

"The peasants working in the fields, the great unhedged fields, looked after him from the distance; and sometimes some sympathetic old woman on the threshold of a low, thatched hut was moved to make the sign of the cross in the air behind his back; as though he were one of themselves, a simple village soul struck by a sore affliction.

"He rode looking straight ahead seeing no one as if the earth were empty and all mankind buried in that grave which had opened so suddenly in his path to swallow up his happiness. What were men to him with their sorrows, joys, labours and passions from which she who had been all the world to him had been cut off so early?

"They did not exist; and he would have felt as completely lonely and abandoned as a man in the toils of a cruel nightmare if it had not been for this countryside where he had been born and had spent his happy boyish years. He knew it well — every slight rise crowned with trees amongst the ploughed fields, every dell concealing a village. The dammed streams made a chain of lakes set in the green meadows. Far away to the north the great Lithuanian forest faced the sun, no higher than a hedge; and to the south, the way to the plains, the vast brown spaces of the earth touched the blue sky.

"And this familiar landscape associated with the days without thought and without sorrow, this land the charm of which he felt without even looking at it soothed his pain, like the presence of an old friend who sits silent and disregarded by one in some dark hour of life.

"One afternoon, it happened that the Prince after turning his horse's head for home remarked a low dense cloud of dark dust cutting off slantwise a part of the view. He reined in on a knoll and peered. There were slender gleams of steel here and there in that cloud, and it contained moving forms which revealed themselves at last as a long line of peasant carts full of soldiers, moving slowly in double file under the escort of mounted Cossacks.

"It was like an immense reptile creeping over the fields; its head dipped out of sight in a slight hollow and its tail went on writhing and growing shorter as though the monster were eating its way slowly into the very heart of the land.

"The Prince directed his way through a village lying a little off the track. The roadside inn with its stable, byre, and barn under one enormous thatched roof resembled a deformed, hunch-backed, ragged giant, sprawling amongst the small huts of the peasants. The innkeeper, a portly, dignified Jew, clad in a black satin coat reaching down to his heels and girt with a red sash, stood at the door stroking his long silvery beard.

"He watched the Prince approach and bowed gravely from the waist, not expecting to be noticed even, since it was well known that their young lord had no eyes for anything or anybody in his grief. It was quite a shock for him when the Prince pulled up and asked:

"'What's all this, Yankel?'

"'That is, please your Serenity, that is a convoy of foot-soldiers they are hurrying down to the south.'

"He glanced right and left cautiously, but as there was no one near but some children playing in the dust of the village street, he came up close to the stirrup.

"'Doesn't your Serenity know? It has begun already down there. All the landowners great and small are out in arms and even the common people have risen. Only yesterday the saddler from Grodek (it was a tiny market-town near by) went through here with his two apprentices on his way to join. He left even his cart with me. I gave him a guide through our neighbourhood. You know, your Serenity, our people they travel a lot and they see all that's going on, and they know all the roads.'

"He tried to keep down his excitement, for the Jew Yankel, innkeeper and tenant of all the mills on the estate, was a Polish patriot. And in a still lower voice:

"'I was already a married man when the French and all the other nations passed this way with Napoleon. Tse! Tse! That was a great harvest for death, nu! Perhaps this time God will help.'

"The Prince nodded. 'Perhaps' — and falling into deep meditation he let his horse take him home.

"That night he wrote a letter, and early in the morning sent a mounted express to the post town. During the day he came out of his taciturnity, to the great joy of the family circle, and conversed with his father of recent events —

the revolt in Warsaw, the flight of the Grand Duke Constantine, the first slight successes of the Polish army (at that time there was a Polish army); the risings in the provinces. Old Prince John, moved and uneasy, speaking from a purely aristocratic point of view, mistrusted the popular origins of the movement, regretted its democratic tendencies, and did not believe in the possibility of success. He was sad, inwardly agitated.

"'I am judging all this calmly. There are secular principles of legitimacy and order which have been violated in this reckless enterprise for the sake of most subversive illusions. Though of course the patriotic impulses of the heart....'

"Prince Roman had listened in a thoughtful attitude. He took advantage of the pause to tell his father quietly that he had sent that morning a letter to St. Petersburg resigning his commission in the Guards.

"The old prince remained silent. He thought that he ought to have been consulted. His son was also ordnance officer to the Emperor and he knew that the Tsar would never forget this appearance of defection in a Polish noble. In a discontented tone he pointed out to his son that as it was he had an unlimited leave. The right thing would have been to keep quiet. They had too much tact at Court to recall a man of his name. Or at worst some distant mission might have been asked for — to the Caucasus for instance — away from this unhappy struggle which was wrong in principle and therefore destined to fail.

"'Presently you shall find yourself without any interest in life and with no occupation. And you shall need something to occupy you, my poor boy. You have acted rashly, I fear.'

"Prince Roman murmured.

"'I thought it better.'

"His father faltered under his steady gaze.

"'Well, well — perhaps! But as ordnance officer to the Emperor and in favour with all the Imperial family....'

"'Those people had never been heard of when our house was already illustrious,' the young man let fall disdainfully.

"This was the sort of remark to which the old prince was sensible.

"'Well — perhaps it is better,' he conceded at last.

"The father and son parted affectionately for the night. The next day Prince Roman seemed to have fallen back into the depths of his indifference. He rode out as usual. He remembered that the day before he had seen a reptile-like convoy of soldiery, bristling with bayonets, crawling over the face of that land which was his. The woman he loved had been his, too. Death had robbed him of her. Her loss had been to him a moral shock. It had opened his heart to a greater sorrow, his mind to a vaster thought, his eyes to all the past and to the existence of another love fraught with pain but as mysteriously imperative as that lost one to which he had entrusted his happiness.

"That evening he retired earlier than usual and rang for his personal servant.

"'Go and see if there is light yet in the quarters of the Master-of-the-Horse. If he is still up ask him to come and speak to me.'

"While the servant was absent on this errand the Prince tore up hastily some papers, locked the drawers of his desk, and hung a medallion, containing the miniature of his wife, round his neck against his breast.

"The man the Prince was expecting belonged to that past which the death of his love had called to life. He was of a family of small nobles who for generations had been adherents, servants, and friends of the Princes S —— — — -. He remembered the times before the last partition and had taken part in the struggles of the last hour. He was a typical old Pole of that class, with a great capacity for emotion, for blind enthusiasm; with martial instincts and simple beliefs; and even with the old-time habit of larding his speech with Latin words. And his kindly shrewd eyes, his ruddy face, his lofty brow and his thick, gray, pendent moustache were also very typical of his kind.

"'Listen, Master Francis,' the Prince said familiarly and without preliminaries. 'Listen, old friend. I am going to vanish from here quietly. I go where something louder than my grief and yet something with a voice very like it calls me. I confide in you alone. You will say what's necessary when the time comes.'

"The old man understood. His extended hands trembled exceedingly. But as soon as he found his voice he thanked God aloud for letting him live long enough to see the descendant of the illustrious family in its youngest generation give an example *coram Gentibus* of the love of his country and of valour in the field. He doubted not of his dear Prince attaining a place in council and in war worthy of his high birth; he saw already that *in fulgore* of family glory *affulget patride serenitas*. At the end of the speech he burst into tears and fell into the Prince's arms.

"The Prince quieted the old man and when he had him seated in an armchair and comparatively composed he said:

"'Don't misunderstand me, Master Francis. You know how I loved my wife. A loss like that opens one's eyes to unsuspected truths. There is no question here of leadership and glory. I mean to go alone and to fight obscurely in the ranks. I am going to offer my country what is mine to offer, that is my life, as simply as the saddler from Grodek who went through yesterday with his apprentices.'

"The old man cried out at this. That could never be. He could not allow it. But he had to give way before the arguments and the express will of the Prince. "'Ha! If you say that it is a matter of feeling and conscience — so be it. But you cannot go utterly alone. Alas! that I am too old to be of any use. *Cripit verba dolor*, my dear Prince, at the thought that I am over seventy and of no more account in the world than a cripple in the church porch. It seems that to sit at home and pray to God for the nation and for you is all I am fit for. But there is my son, my youngest son, Peter. He will make a worthy companion for you. And as it happens he's staying with me here. There has not been for ages a Prince S —— —— - hazarding his life without a companion of our name to ride by his side. You must have by you somebody who knows who you are if only to let your parents and your old servant hear what is happening to you. And when does your Princely Mightiness mean to start?'

"'In an hour,' said the Prince; and the old man hurried off to warn his son.

"Prince Roman took up a candlestick and walked quietly along a dark corridor in the silent house. The head-nurse said afterwards that waking up suddenly she saw the Prince looking at his child, one hand shading the light from its eyes. He stood and gazed at her for some time, and then putting the candlestick on the floor bent over the cot and kissed lightly the little girl who did not wake. He went out noiselessly, taking the light away with him. She saw his face perfectly well, but she could read nothing of his purpose in it. It was pale but perfectly calm and after he turned away from the cot he never looked back at it once.

"The only other trusted person, besides the old man and his son Peter, was the Jew Yankel. When he asked the Prince where precisely he wanted to be guided the Prince answered: 'To the nearest party.' A grandson of the Jew, a lanky youth, conducted the two young men by little-known paths across woods and morasses, and led them in sight of the few fires of a small detachment camped in a hollow. Some invisible horses neighed, a voice in the dark cried: 'Who goes there?'... and the young Jew departed hurriedly, explaining that he must make haste home to be in time for keeping the Sabbath.

"Thus humbly and in accord with the simplicity of the vision of duty he saw when death had removed the brilliant bandage of happiness from his eyes, did Prince Roman bring his offering to his country. His companion made himself known as the son of the Master of-the-Horse to the Princes S —— —— - and declared him to be a relation, a distant cousin from the same parts as himself and, as people presumed, of the same name. In truth no one inquired much. Two more young men clearly of the right sort had joined. Nothing more natural.

"Prince Roman did not remain long in the south. One day while scouting with several others, they were ambushed near the entrance of a village by some Russian infantry. The first discharge laid low a good many and the rest scattered in all directions. The Russians, too, did not stay, being afraid of a return in force. After some time, the peasants coming to view the scene extricated Prince Roman from under his dead horse. He was unhurt but his faithful companion had been one of the first to fall. The Prince helped the peasants to bury him and the other dead.

"Then alone, not certain where to find the body of partizans which was constantly moving about in all directions, he resolved to try and join the main Polish army facing the Russians on the borders of Lithuania. Disguised in peasant clothes, in case of meeting some marauding Cossacks, he wandered a couple of weeks before he came upon a village occupied by a regiment of Polish cavalry on outpost duty.

"On a bench, before a peasant hut of a better sort, sat an elderly officer whom he took for the colonel. The Prince approached respectfully, told his story shortly and stated his desire to enlist; and when asked his name by the officer, who had been looking him over carefully, he gave on the spur of the moment the name of his dead companion.

"The elderly officer thought to himself: Here's the son of some peasant proprietor of the liberated class. He liked his appearance.

"'And can you read and write, my good fellow?'he asked.

"'Yes, your honour, I can,' said the Prince.

"'Good. Come along inside the hut; the regimental adjutant is there. He will enter your name and administer the oath to you.'

"The adjutant stared very hard at the newcomer but said nothing. When all the forms had been gone through and the recruit gone out, he turned to his superior officer.

"'Do you know who that is?'

"'Who? That Peter? A likely chap.'

"'That's Prince Roman S —— —— -.'

"'Nonsense.'

"But the adjutant was positive. He had seen the Prince several times, about two years before, in the Castle in Warsaw. He had even spoken to him once at a reception of officers held by the Grand Duke.

"'He's changed. He seems much older, but I am certain of my man. I have a good memory for faces.'

"The two officers looked at each other in silence.

"'He's sure to be recognized sooner or later,' murmured the adjutant. The colonel shrugged his shoulders.

"'It's no affair of ours — if he has a fancy to serve in the ranks. As to being recognized it's not so likely. All our officers and men come from the other end of Poland.'

"He meditated gravely for a while, then smiled. 'He told me he could read and write. There's nothing to prevent me making him a sergeant at the first opportunity. He's sure to shape all right.'

"Prince Roman as a non-commissioned officer surpassed the colonel's expectations. Before long Sergeant Peter became famous for his resourcefulness and courage. It was not the reckless courage of a desperate man; it was a self-possessed, as if conscientious, valour which nothing could dismay; a boundless but equable devotion, unaffected by time, by reverses, by the discouragement of endless retreats, by the bitterness of waning hopes and the horrors of pestilence added to the toils and perils of war. It was in this year that the cholera made its first appearance in Europe. It devastated the camps of both armies, affecting the firmest minds with the terror of a mysterious death stalking silently between the piled-up arms and around the bivouac fires.

"A sudden shriek would wake up the harassed soldiers and they would see in the glow of embers one of themselves writhe on the ground like a worm trodden on by an invisible foot. And before the dawn broke he would be stiff and cold. Parties so visited have been known to rise like one man, abandon the fire and run off into the night in mute panic. Or a comrade talking to you on the march would stammer suddenly in the middle of a sentence, roll affrighted eyes, and fall down with distorted face and blue lips, breaking the ranks with the convulsions of his agony. Men were struck in the saddle, on sentry duty, in the firing line, carrying orders, serving the guns. I have been told that in a battalion forming under fire with perfect steadiness for the assault of a village, three cases occurred within five minutes at the head of the column; and the attack could not be delivered because the leading companies scattered all over the fields like chaff before the wind.

"Sergeant Peter, young as he was, had a great influence over his men. It was said that the number of desertions in the squadron in which he served was less than in any other in the whole of that cavalry division. Such was supposed to be the compelling example of one man's quiet intrepidity in facing every form of danger and terror.

"However that may be, he was liked and trusted generally. When the end came and the remnants of that army corps, hard pressed on all sides, were preparing to cross the Prussian frontier, Sergeant Peter had enough influence to rally round him a score of troopers. He managed to escape with them at night, from the hemmed-in army. He led this band through 200 miles of country covered by numerous Russian detachments and ravaged by the cholera. But this was not to avoid captivity, to go into hiding and try to save themselves. No. He led them into a fortress which was still occupied by the Poles, and where the last stand of the vanquished revolution was to be made.

"This looks like mere fanaticism. But fanaticism is human. Man has adored ferocious divinities. There is ferocity in every passion, even in love itself. The religion of undying hope resembles the mad cult of despair, of death, of annihilation. The difference lies in the moral motive springing from the secret needs and the unexpressed aspiration of the believers. It is only to vain men that all is vanity; and all is deception only to those who have never been sincere with themselves.

"It was in the fortress that my grandfather found himself together with Sergeant Peter. My grandfather was a neighbour of the S —— —— - family in the country but he did not know Prince Roman, who however knew his name perfectly well. The Prince introduced himself one night as they both sat on the ramparts, leaning against a gun carriage.

"The service he wished to ask for was, in case of his being killed, to have the intelligence conveyed to his parents.

"They talked in low tones, the other servants of the piece lying about near them. My grandfather gave the required promise, and then asked frankly — for he was greatly interested by the disclosure so unexpectedly made:

"But tell me, Prince, why this request? Have you any evil forebodings as to yourself?'

"Not in the least; I was thinking of my people. They have no idea where I am,' answered Prince Roman. 'I'll engage to do as much for you, if you like. It's certain that half of us at least shall be killed before the end, so there's an even chance of one of us surviving the other.'

"My grandfather told him where, as he supposed, his wife and children were then. From that moment till the end of the siege the two were much together. On the day of the great assault my grandfather received a severe wound. The town was taken. Next day the citadel itself, its hospital full of dead and dying, its magazines empty, its defenders having burnt their last cartridge, opened its gates.

"During all the campaign the Prince, exposing his person conscientiously on every occasion, had not received a scratch. No one had recognized him or at any rate had betrayed his identity. Till then, as long as he did his duty, it had mattered nothing who he was.

"Now, however, the position was changed. As ex-guardsman and as late ordnance officer to the Emperor, this rebel ran a serious risk of being given special attention in the shape of a firing squad at ten paces. For more than a month he remained lost in the miserable crowd of prisoners packed in the casemates of the citadel, with just enough food to keep body and soul together but otherwise allowed to die from wounds, privation, and disease at the rate of forty or so a day.

"The position of the fortress being central, new parties, captured in the open in the course of a thorough pacification, were being sent in frequently. Amongst such new-comers there happened to be a young man, a personal friend of the Prince from his school days. He recognized him, and in the extremity of his dismay cried aloud: 'My God! Roman, you here!'

"It is said that years of life embittered by remorse paid for this momentary lack of self-control. All this happened in the main quadrangle of the citadel. The warning gesture of the Prince came too late. An officer of the gendarmes on guard had heard the exclamation. The incident appeared to him worth inquiring into. The investigation which followed was not very arduous because the Prince, asked categorically for his real name, owned up at once.

"The intelligence of the Prince S —— —— — being found amongst the prisoners was sent to St. Petersburg. His parents were already there living in sorrow, incertitude, and apprehension. The capital of the Empire was the safest place to reside in for a noble whose son had disappeared so mysteriously from home in a time of rebellion. The old people had not heard from him, or of him, for months. They took care not to contradict the rumours of suicide from despair circulating in the great world, which remembered the interesting love-match, the charming and frank happiness brought to an end by death. But they hoped secretly that their son survived, and that he had been able to cross the frontier with that part of the army which had surrendered to the Prussians.

"The news of his captivity was a crushing blow. Directly, nothing could be done for him. But the greatness of their name, of their position, their wide relations and connections in the highest spheres, enabled his parents to act indirectly and they moved heaven and earth, as the saying is, to save their son from the 'consequences of his madness,' as poor Prince John did not hesitate to express himself. Great personages were approached by society leaders, high dignitaries were interviewed, powerful officials were induced to take an interest in that affair. The help of every possible secret influence was enlisted. Some private secretaries got heavy bribes. The mistress of a certain senator obtained a large sum of money.

"But, as I have said, in such a glaring case no direct appeal could be made and no open steps taken. All that could be done was to incline by private representation the mind of the President of the Military Commission to the side of clemency. He ended by being impressed by the hints and suggestions, some of them from very high quarters, which he received from St. Petersburg. And, after all, the gratitude of such great nobles as the Princes S ——
—— was something worth having from a worldly point of view. He was a good Russian but he was also a good-natured man. Moreover, the hate of Poles was not at that time a cardinal article of patriotic creed as it became some thirty years later. He felt well disposed at first sight towards that young man, bronzed, thin-faced, worn out by months of hard campaigning, the hardships of the siege and the rigours of captivity.

"The Commission was composed of three officers. It sat in the citadel in a bare vaulted room behind a long black table. Some clerks occupied the two ends, and besides the gendarmes who brought in the Prince there was no one else there.

"Within those four sinister walls shutting out from him all the sights and sounds of liberty, all hopes of the future, all consoling illusions — alone in the face of his enemies erected for judges, who can tell how much love of life there was in Prince Roman? How much remained in that sense of duty, revealed to him in sorrow? How much of his awakened love for his native country? That country which demands to be loved as no other country has ever been loved, with the mournful affection one bears to the unforgotten dead and with the unextinguishable fire of a hopeless passion which only a living, breathing, warm ideal can kindle in our breasts for our pride, for our weariness, for our exultation, for our undoing.

"There is something monstrous in the thought of such an exaction till it stands before us embodied in the shape of a fidelity without fear and without reproach. Nearing the supreme moment of his life the Prince could only have had the feeling that it was about to end. He answered the questions put to him clearly, concisely — with the most profound indifference. After all those tense months of action, to talk was a weariness to him. But he concealed it, lest his foes should suspect in his manner the apathy of discouragement or the numbness of a crushed spirit. The details of his conduct could have no importance one way or another; with his thoughts these men had nothing to do. He preserved a scrupulously courteous tone. He had refused the permission to sit down.

"What happened at this preliminary examination is only known from the presiding officer. Pursuing the only possible course in that glaringly bad case he tried from the first to bring to the Prince's mind the line of defence he wished him to take. He absolutely framed his questions so as to put the right answers in the culprit's mouth, going so far as to suggest the very words: how, distracted by excessive grief after his young wife's death, rendered irresponsible for his conduct by his despair, in a moment of blind recklessness, without realizing the highly reprehensible nature of the act, nor yet its danger and its dishonour, he went off to join the nearest rebels on a sudden impulse. And that now, penitently...

"But Prince Roman was silent. The military judges looked at him hopefully. In silence he reached for a pen and wrote on a sheet of paper he found under his hand: 'I joined the national rising from conviction.'

"He pushed the paper across the table. The president took it up, showed it in turn to his two colleagues sitting to the right and left, then looking fixedly at Prince Roman let it fall from his hand. And the silence remained unbroken till he spoke to the gendarmes ordering them to remove the prisoner.

"Such was the written testimony of Prince Roman in the supreme moment of his life. I have heard that the Princes of the S —— —— - family, in all its branches, adopted the last two words: 'From conviction' for the device under the armorial bearings of their house. I don't know whether the report is true. My uncle could not tell me. He remarked only, that naturally, it was not to be seen on Prince Roman's own seal.

"He was condemned for life to Siberian mines. Emperor Nicholas, who always took personal cognizance of all sentences on Polish nobility, wrote with his own hand in the margin: 'The authorities are severely warned to take care that this convict walks in chains like any other criminal every step of the way.'

"It was a sentence of deferred death. Very few survived entombment in these mines for more than three years. Yet as he was reported as still alive at the end of that time he was allowed, on a petition of his parents and by way of exceptional grace, to serve as common soldier in the Caucasus. All communication with him was forbidden. He had no civil rights. For all practical purposes except that of suffering he was a dead man. The little child he had been so careful not to wake up when he kissed her in her cot, inherited all the fortune after Prince John's death.

Her existence saved those immense estates from confiscation.

"It was twenty-five years before Prince Roman, stone deaf, his health broken, was permitted to return to Poland. His daughter married splendidly to a Polish Austrian *grand seigneur* and, moving in the cosmopolitan sphere of the highest European aristocracy, lived mostly abroad in Nice and Vienna. He, settling down on one of her estates, not the one with the palatial residence but another where there was a modest little house, saw very little of her.

"But Prince Roman did not shut himself up as if his work were done. There was hardly anything done in the private and public life of the neighbourhood, in which Prince Roman's advice and assistance were not called upon, and never in vain. It was well said that his days did not belong to himself but to his fellow citizens. And especially he was the particular friend of all returned exiles, helping them with purse and advice, arranging their affairs and finding them means of livelihood.

"I heard from my uncle many tales of his devoted activity, in which he was always guided by a simple wisdom, a high sense of honour, and the most scrupulous conception of private and public probity. He remains a living figure for me because of that meeting in a billiard room, when, in my anxiety to hear about a particularly wolfish wolf, I came in momentary contact with a man who was preeminently a man amongst all men capable of feeling deeply, of believing steadily, of loving ardently.

"I remember to this day the grasp of Prince Roman's bony, wrinkled hand closing on my small inky paw, and my uncle's half-serious, half-amused way of looking down at his trespassing nephew.

"They moved on and forgot that little boy. But I did not move; I gazed after them, not so much disappointed as disconcerted by this prince so utterly unlike a prince in a fairy tale. They moved very slowly across the room. Before reaching the other door the Prince stopped, and I heard him — I seem to hear him now — saying: 'I wish you would write to Vienna about filling up that post. He's a most deserving fellow — and your recommendation would be decisive.'

"My uncle's face turned to him expressed genuine wonder. It said as plainly as any speech could say: What better recommendation than a father's can be needed? The Prince was quick at reading expressions. Again he spoke with the toneless accent of a man who has not heard his own voice for years, for whom the soundless world is like an abode of silent shades.

"And to this day I remember the very words: 'I ask you because, you see, my daughter and my son-in-law don't believe me to be a good judge of men. They think that I let myself be guided too much by mere sentiment.'"

Made in the USA
Columbia, SC
15 October 2024

44441125R00024